BLAST OFF

IF YOU DARE!

STORIES FROM SPACE MOUNTAIN

by Cathy East Dubowski

DISNEY
PRESS

NEW YORK

Printed in the United States of America.

FIRST EDITION
1 3 5 7 9 10 8 6 4 2

Library of Congress Cataloging-in-Publication Data
Dubowski, Cathy East.
Blast off if you dare! stories from Space Mountain / by Cathy East Dubowski. — 1st ed.
p.   cm.
Contents: The ride of your life—Scouts honor—My little sister is a real brat!—Home sweet home—Freaks.
ISBN 0-7868-4107-9 (pbk.)
1. Science fiction, American.   2. Children's stories, American.
[1. Science fiction.   2. Short stories.]   I. Title.
PZ7.D8544Br   1997
[Fic]—dc20   96-38222

BLAST OFF

IF YOU DARE!

STORIES FROM SPACE MOUNTAIN

Contents

THE RIDE OF YOUR LIFE

"Come on, Roger, you've got to ride it!"

"It'll be the ride of your life!"

"Yeah," I shot back. "But if I get on it, I might not have a life!"

My friends Mark and Lauren were bugging me to ride Space Mountain.

But I hadn't been on a roller coaster since I was six.

That one was called the Drop of Doom. It hadn't looked so bad from the ground. But as soon as our little log car splashed to a stop at the end of the ride, I threw up cotton candy, popcorn, and soda all over my mom. She swore she was never going to get on one of those rides with me ever again.

She didn't have to worry. I stuck to the merry-go-round after that.

"Chicken!" Mark teased.

Oooh! I hate it when people call me that. Especially somebody like Mark. He's not scared of anything—careening down steep hills on Rollerblades or watching scary movies. Not even cemeteries at midnight scare him. Sometimes I think he must have been *born* on a roller coaster.

And Lauren is just as bad. She looks so sweet and innocent with her big blue eyes and curly blond hair. But don't let that fool you. "Come on," she urged me. "I dare you!"

"Maybe later," I said. "The line's too long right now."

"It's always long, brainless," Mark replied. "It's the most popular ride in the whole park!"

"Get it?" Lauren added. "It's popular because everybody loves it."

I shrugged. "Well, I'm not everybody."

"Look at that little kid over there." Lauren pointed at a small boy standing in line. He looked about five or six and he was sucking his thumb. "Are you going to let a little kid like that show you up?"

She grabbed my arm and started pulling me toward the ride.

I grabbed hold of a lamppost and hung on. I knew I looked ridiculous. But I didn't want to go.

"Hold it!" Mark held up his camera. "I'm going to take a picture of you—Roger Johnson—*not* riding Space Mountain. Then I can show everybody back home what a chicken you were."

Click! The camera caught me in the act.

Mark was laughing. "Now flap your arms up and down and say *Bwaak! Bwaak! Bwaaaak!* I want another shot!"

I couldn't take it anymore.

Their nagging was going to ruin the whole day. Besides, I had to get that picture back. I couldn't risk letting Mark show it to Heather Somerfield back home.

"All right, all right—I'll get on the ride!" I shouted as I hid my face in my hands. "If you let me have that picture."

"Deal!" Mark said. He and Lauren laughed.

"And you've got to ride with me," I added. "But don't blame me if I throw up on you!"

We stood in line on the curved walkway that led up into the towering Space Mountain. The line was long, but I was surprised at how quickly it moved.

Too quickly! I wished the line were longer. Maybe the park would close before I made it onto the ride!

We watched this pretty cool video they had playing on several TV screens to entertain us while we waited in line. A technician from "Space Mountain Mission

Control" flashed on to inform us that our "spaceship" was almost ready. Then he switched to a commercial.

"Hello!" a guy in a silver space suit and tie shouted. "Crazy Larry here, of Crazy Larry's Used Spaceships and Satellites! Hey—are you in the market for a used spaceship? I've got 'em all. I've got rockets, saucers, thrusters, and boosters. I've got photon drives and neutrino drives. All right here under one roof. All with low, low mileage and ready to *blast off* the lot!"

A home shopping channel offered jewelry from the planet Zirconium, and another ad told about an alien aspirin-free pain reliever.

Mark and Lauren and I laughed. And laughing helped calm my nerves. But as the line moved closer, and I began to see people actually getting on the ride, my heart began to pound. My hands felt clammy and my stomach churned.

Don't think about it, I told myself. When the time comes, just get on. Close your eyes. It'll be over in minutes.

What's the worst that could happen? I thought. It was early in the day. I hadn't eaten enough to throw up.

Soon there were only a few people in front of us.

I was glad I had worn Arrid Extra Dry deodorant that morning. Otherwise, my Goofy T-shirt would have been soaked with sweat. And I was getting a headache from clenching my teeth.

"Next!" A girl in a space-age uniform waved us forward.

The cars were shaped like rocket ships. Three people

sat in a row in each car, and there were two cars hooked together.

Mark and Lauren climbed into the last two seats. But there was no room for me. "Hey!" I cried. "You promised you'd ride with me!"

Mark shrugged. "What can I say? Everybody's gotta ride Space Mountain the first time by themselves. It's awesome that way."

"Besides," Lauren called, "it's so dark in there, you won't even notice we're not with you!"

"We'll be waiting for you at the exit!" Mark hollered.

"Yeah—with a stretcher!" Lauren added.

Then their car jerked forward, toward the mouth of a dark tunnel.

Before I could say any more, the space girl called out "Next!" and led me to the next set of cars.

Oh no! Not the front car! I just stood there, staring. My feet felt frozen to the floor. I couldn't get on—I just couldn't!

The space girl cleared her throat. "Step inside, please."

I glanced sideways at her. She was pretty cute. I'd feel like a total nerd to back out now in front of a cool-looking girl like that.

The people behind me were impatient to get on. I was holding up the ride.

I took a deep breath and I crossed my fingers. Then, with a shaky sigh, I climbed into the snug-fitting space car. The cute girl lowered the safety bar in front of me till it locked in place. "Have fun!" she said and she winked at me.

"Yeah, right." I rolled my eyes. Then, as my car suddenly jerked forward toward the darkened tunnel, I whispered to myself, "Blast off . . . if you dare!"

Instantly we plunged down a long dark tunnel—it took my breath away!—and then we flew around a sharp curve as strobe lights flashed like stars. The wind blew my hair straight back, and I was glad my sunglasses were tucked away in my fanny pack. I held on in a death grip through the sharp turns, curves, and dives. All around me I heard people squealing and screaming in delight. But I couldn't scream. I was too scared. And I couldn't help it—I kept my eyes squeezed shut. Maybe if I didn't look, it wouldn't be so scary!

But after a few minutes I began to relax a little. In fact, I even tried keeping my eyes open!

Hey, I'm doing it! I thought. I'm riding a roller coaster! Maybe it was all in my head because of that time I lost my cookies on the Drop of Doom. Maybe I'd outgrown my phobia. Some of the curves were actually fun. And there weren't too many of those awful zero-gravity drops where you plunge straight down and your stomach winds up in your throat.

But then suddenly the whole ride trembled as if there was an earthquake. A bright red light exploded right in front of my eyes, blinding me for a moment.

What was that? I wondered.

I suddenly felt hot and sweaty, as if the air-conditioning had suddenly shut down. What felt like steamy hot breath blasted down my neck.

A high piercing sound sent shivers down my back as

12

I squeezed my eyes shut and felt the wild vibrations of the metal car rattle my bones and teeth. I was scared the car might rattle right off the track!

Then something really weird happened.

As my car sped faster and faster, I felt an odd frightening sensation—hard to describe. Kind of like . . . like all my atoms smooshing through a screen door into another dimension.

My friends never told me about this part!

I felt sick. Not carsick. Not seasick. Space sick!

I closed my eyes and ducked my head into my shoulders and held on to the fat safety bar as the car shook like crazy.

I screamed, "I want to get off! Please! Please let me get off!"

I don't know how long I stayed hunched over against the safety bar. It seemed like hours.

And then, at last, I felt the ride slowing down.

It was almost over. I'd made it—in one piece!

The ride shuddered to a stop.

I sat still a moment, gasping, with my eyes clenched tight, waiting for all my internal organs to settle back into their proper places inside my body. Waiting for my pounding heart to slow down from ABSOLUTE TERROR to only MILDLY FREAKED OUT.

Finally, I sighed in relief.

A large part of fear, after all, is fear of the unknown. Not knowing what's going to happen next—or how long it's going to last. Now I knew what the ride was like. I knew the boundaries. I had ridden into the unknown—I had faced a childhood fear—and survived.

It was scary, but I was all right.

I felt a small rush of excitement and pride.

I did it! I rode Space Mountain—without throwing up!

I sighed again and opened my eyes. As I climbed out of the metal spaceship car, I looked around the exit dock for Mark and Lauren. It seemed awfully quiet.

In fact, it seemed . . . totally deserted.

Hey—where is everybody?

I shrugged. I guessed I'd sat there longer than I realized. I better hurry. I might be holding up the ride.

I took a shaky step, gasping and laughing a little, trying to get my bearings. I was a little dizzy from the ride. Just a little wobbly.

I started to walk, but I felt as if I were wearing cement sneakers. I could barely move my feet. It was almost as if extra gravity were tugging me toward the ground.

At first I was frightened.

But then I thought: Must be a special effect—triple Earth gravity or something. Amazing. I wondered how they did that.

At the exit, dazzling light blinded me—almost as if there were two suns blazing down.

At last I could see a couple of vague shapes silhouetted in the glare. I figured it was Mark and Lauren.

I wished I could throw up on them. That would teach them for leaving me in a car all by myself!

"How was the trip?" one said.

"Not so terrible, now, was it?" said the other.

"Piece of cake," I lied as I staggered toward them.

I still couldn't see them in the blinding light.

But their voices sounded odd. Eerie. It was almost as if the sound were coming through a garbage disposal. Maybe my ears were clogged up, like when you drive up into the mountains or take off in an airplane.

I rubbed at my ears as I squinted into the light. I staggered toward them and one of them reached out for my hand.

"Steady now."

I shrieked and jerked my hand away.

What I had touched was not the warm soft flesh of a human hand but something cold and slimy, like wet rubber.

I looked at my hand.

My palm and fingers were coated with glowing aqua slime.

I looked up with narrowed eyes. I was getting used to the bright light. And then I saw . . .

15

Not Mark and Lauren.

Not even other human beings.

I was looking at creatures unlike any I'd ever seen before—even in my worst nightmares.

Monsters.

Aliens!

I choked back a scream.

Wait, calm down! I told myself frantically, fighting the panic. It must be special effects. Actors . . . mirrors . . . Animatronic robot things . . .

I'd almost convinced myself.

I tried to shove past these monsters. All I wanted to do was find my friends. Maybe a few dozen rides on the "It's a Small World" ride would calm me down.

But the creatures blocked my path with their huge bulky shapes. I felt their slimy tentacles wrap like snakes around my arms.

I felt as if I weighed three hundred pounds. I couldn't run. I couldn't break away.

And then they led me away from the ride, while my eyes searched frantically for my friends. Where were the crowds? Where were the souvenir stands? Where were the other attractions?

Where were my friends when I needed them?

But I saw nothing I recognized. The landscape before me stretched endlessly to a rust-colored sky. The ground churned like molten mud. Green mists that smelled like diesel exhaust wafted across the landscape.

This was too large to be a set, too unreal to be virtual reality.

Terror turned my bones to jelly as I realized: This is real!

Fear rose in my throat like bile. I knew I was no longer in any theme park. And I knew my friends were not there to greet me . . . or save me.

Something had gone wrong.

Somehow my car on the roller coaster had crashed through some barrier of time and space—

And delivered me to an alien planet.

Was it an accident? Or had the aliens somehow captured me and brought me here on purpose?

What would Mark and Lauren do when I didn't get off the ride? Had this ever happened to any other riders? Or was I the lucky one? *Ha!*

More important, was there any way to get back?

"Welllllcome," one creature rasped, drooling on my arm.

"Yes, earthling," the second one said, smacking his huge hairy lips. "And now, we'd like to have you for dinner."

I had a feeling I was not the honored guest, to be pampered and treated like visiting royalty.

I had a feeling I was going to be the main course.

SCOUT'S HONOR

"Wh-what was that?"

Adam Little looked around the unfamiliar planet.

"It's the boogeyman," Brad Mooser said. "And you better watch out, Little, because the boogeyman loves chicken!"

Brad and his pals laughed.

"Hey," Brad said. "That's it! Adam's new nick-name—Chicken Little!"

"Cut it out, Brad," Ylana Sylvian snapped. She and Adam were building the huge campfire the scouts would use to cook dinner. To Adam, she added, "Just ignore him. He's just being a jerk."

"Well, at least I'm not scared of a measly little old camping trip," Brad jeered before heading off with his pals to search for more firewood.

Adam was the newest member of Scout Troop 2000, and he'd never even been away from home—the exploration starship *Euphoria*—much less gone camping on an unsettled planet like Botania-9.

Botania-9 was the newest of several thousand undeveloped planets across the galaxy that had been set aside as international parkland.

Adam couldn't believe how big it was, how the land went on and on to the horizon. It was a beautiful planet. Lush plant life covered the terrain as far as the eye could see. Thick green plants reached toward the sky. Rushing streams and sparkling lakes ran clean and pollution-free. But no signs of animal life—not even bugs.

As the sky darkened that evening, and the temperature dropped, Adam grew nervous. This fire they were building—Adam had never seen fire before. It was beautiful and warm, but it cast strange leaping shadows around their campsite.

The starship *Euphoria* was never completely dark. For efficiency, the crew and passengers worked in shifts around the clock, so that even during Adam's night period, lights remained on in other parts of the starship.

Besides, his mother preferred to dim the lights only to level two. And if Adam woke up, he could switch on the lights with a wave of his hand.

But here—man, it got *dark*! Adam glanced around the clearing surrounded by huge waving plants. He'd never realized just how black darkness could be.

"You'll get used to it," Ylana said.

"Huh?"

Ylana grinned. "The darkness. It really freaked me out on my first camping trip, too. We camped out on Fluvynia IV, and I didn't sleep a wink the first night. But you do get used to it."

Adam pulled a small can out of his backpack and began to spray it on his arms and legs.

"Whew!" Brad hollered. "What's that awful stink! Hey, Chicken Little. You wearing cologne out here?"

"No way!" Adam replied. "It's insect repellent. My parents made me promise to wear it, just in case."

"I don't see any bugs. Do you see any bugs?" Brad asked his buddy Zedron.

"Yeah, well, you're bugging us," Ylana shot back. "So buzz off!"

Brad and his pals laughed as they wandered off.

"Thanks," Adam said sheepishly.

"Don't mention it," Ylana said.

At suppertime the troop gathered around the fire. Adam was amazed to watch the scouts who were in charge of dinner actually cook their stew in a cast-iron pot suspended over the fire.

Food on the *Euphoria* came from a central processing station and arrived at regular intervals in his family's dining cubicle. He'd never thought about how it got cooked.

"Ah, this is the life," their scoutmaster, Mr. Gordon, said as he sat down with his plate of stew. "This is the way we did it on Earth when I was a small boy. My dad and uncle used to take me camping in the mountains, where we'd spend the whole day fishing."

Adam wanted to ask what fishing was, but he didn't want to sound stupid.

After dinner the scouts made an old-fashioned dessert that Mr. Gordon remembered from when he was on Earth—S'mores. It was very special, since all the ingredients had to be imported from Earth and were very expensive. The recipe called for layering a thin chocolate bar and a fire-toasted marshmallow in between two graham cracker squares.

"These are great!" Adam mumbled around a mouthful.

Ylana nodded and wiped melted chocolate from her lips. "My grandmother makes these sometimes for special occasions."

"Hey, how about a ghost story!" Brad called out.

"Yeah!" several of the kids agreed.

"I got one," Brad said. "It's called 'The Bloody Tentacle.'"

"That's a good one!" his buddy Zedron said. "Tell it!"

"Well," Brad began, leaning toward the fire, "it all

started one dark rainy night, on the planet Ngovian. A boy was walking his girlfriend home from a party. Suddenly, up ahead, they saw lights glowing through the darkness. At first they thought it was hovercraft headlights, but as they walked toward the lights, they realized that the lights were eyes!"

Adam squirmed. He liked reading ghost stories in his bunk back home, with his mom and dad in the next room.

But here in the dark wilderness, with no walls or roof around him, no automatic lights or security systems, everything was a whole lot scarier.

As Brad continued his story, the scouts leaned toward him, hanging on every word. A few kids looked as spooked as Adam.

Adam was getting goose bumps. He glanced around the darkness. It seemed as if the towering treelike plants had inched closer and closer to the fire. And there—behind Brad's head—something was glowing in the darkness.

Eyes!

Something was out there!

"Look!" Adam cried, jumping up and dropping his S'more to the ground. "Something's out there in the woods!"

A few kids screamed. Everyone jumped up and stared out into the night.

But the eyes Adam had seen were gone.

"Where?" a girl named Halley cried. "I don't see anything."

Brad snorted. "Yeah, that's because there isn't anything out there." He glared at Adam. "Hey, I think we ought to put the babies to bed before we tell any more ghost stories."

"All right, Brad, cut it out," Mr. Gordon said. "That's not good scoutsmanship."

Adam's face burned with embarrassment. "Well, there was something out there. I saw it."

Mr. Gordon patted Adam on the shoulder. "Don't worry, son. Your eyes aren't used to firelight. Sometimes when we stare at a bright light like this, then glance out into the darkness, our eyes can play tricks on us and make us think we see things. Things that aren't really there. The scoutmaster chuckled. "That's probably the way most of these ghost stories get started in the first place." Then he looked Adam in the eyes. "You okay?" he asked gently. "Want us to stop telling stories?"

Adam looked around at his troop mates. All the kids would make fun of him if he said yes. He'd never live it down. He tried to smile. "No, that's OK, I'm fine! Let's keep going."

Brad finished his story. Then others took a turn. The stories ranged from ancient stories of ghosts and pirates on Earth to terrifying tales from other galaxies. When things got too spooky, Adam would only pretend to listen and instead would fill his mind with other things, like counting backward from a hundred.

Soon Mr. Gordon stood up and stretched. "Time

for some shut-eye, kids. The sun comes up around 0400 here, so we'd best get to sleep."

Adam and the others quickly pulled out their gear and unrolled their sleeping bags. They were similar to the sleep sacs they slept in on the *Euphoria*, only here they spread them out on the ground instead of in a bunk.

Then Adam realized he was in trouble. He'd drunk a lot of soda at suppertime, and now he knew he couldn't put it off. He'd have to hike off to the portable waste disposal vacuum cabinet they'd set up in the woods.

"Anybody need to take a hike?" he asked, forcing himself to sound cheerful.

A few kids shook their heads.

"Need somebody to hold your hand, Chicken Little?" Brad sneered.

Adam ignored him and took off down the path.

Jumping Jupiter, but it was dark, he thought. If it hadn't been for the pale light from Botania-9's two quarter moons, he wouldn't have been able to see his hand in front of his face.

He flicked on his laserflash and trained the beam on the path before him. Twisted roots crisscrossed the path like writhing snakes.

He thought he saw something glowing off to the side. Then he thought he heard a muttering noise.

Don't look, he told himself. Just hurry and take care of business and get back to the others.

He dashed into the portable waste disposal vacuum cabinet. Minutes later he was dashing back up the trail

toward the comforting light of the campfire.

Along the path he thought he heard eerie rustlings in the thick vegetation, as if somebody—or something—were walking toward him. He thought he heard whispering among the treelike plants. He was sure he saw strange dots of greenish glowing light—and this time he hadn't been staring at the campfire.

He raced back to camp.

"Mr. Gordon, I-I—" He broke off when he saw the other campers staring at him.

But he had to speak up. There might really be something out there—something dangerous!

"What is it, Adam?" Mr. Gordon asked.

"I-I heard something out in the woods," he stuttered. "Rustling—like somebody was walking around. And I saw these lights glowing—they looked like eyes—and I hadn't been staring at the fire."

Brad smirked and rolled his eyes, but Adam kept going. "I know it sounds crazy, Mr. Gordon, but I think there's something out there."

"Mr. Gordon, I'm scared!" Halley cried.

A few other kids agreed, but most joined Brad in making fun of Adam.

"OK, everybody, settle down," Mr. Gordon said. He pulled out his bioscope and flicked it on, then walked to the edge of the campfire and aimed it out into the night. The device beeped quietly and steadily as he scanned the darkness, walking a complete circle around the campfire. Dancing firelight made eerie shadows flicker across the scoutmaster's back.

Adam held his breath.

When Mr. Gordon finally circled the entire camp-fire, he turned to Adam. "My readings indicate that there's absolutely no sign of any animal life of any kind—people, animals, insects—within a three-hundred-mile radius of our camp. Nothing. Zip. It's highly unlikely that anything exists beyond that, either, and even if it did, it would be no threat to us tonight."

"Are—are you sure?" Adam said.

The scoutmaster nodded. "Now, why don't we all get some sleep?"

Adam glanced around at his fellow scouts. Everyone else seemed satisfied by the scoutmaster's report.

Even Ylana. "Hey, it's all right," she said, slapping him on the back. "It's just normal first-night jitters. Get some sleep. You'll feel a whole lot different in the morning."

"Yeah, definitely," Adam mumbled. But he wasn't so sure.

Soon everyone had snuggled down in their podlike sleeping bags. The night was cold, and the sky grew darker as their blazing campfire burned down to glow-ing coals.

Adam curled up in his sleeping bag and stared at the night sky, too nervous to sleep. Quit being such a baby, he scolded himself. But he couldn't help it.

He tried searching the sky for his favorite constella-tion, Orion. There it was! And to the right of it he spotted the starship *Euphoria*, appearing not much larger than a star itself.

Adam wished he were there now, sleeping warm and safe in his own bed, with his parents and his older sister nearby. If he ever lived through this night, he'd never go off-ship again.

He dozed. Then suddenly he started—he could have sworn he heard footsteps, soft shuffling footsteps, coming closer and closer . . .

"What was that?" he yelped.

"Shut up, jerk!" Brad yelled at him. "Some of us are trying to sleep!"

"Everything's OK, Adam," Mr. Gordon called over in his deep soothing voice. "I was the same way on my first sleep-out under the stars. Just relax. Take some deep breaths, and you'll fall asleep. Everything's fine, just fine. I promise."

At last Adam began to feel sleepy. Soon all was quiet. The only sounds were the occasional pop of the dying campfire, two or three scouts snoring . . . somebody mumbling in a dream . . .

Adam drifted off into an uneasy sleep.

Adam woke up. He thought he heard a rustling sound, muffled voices.

It's nothing! he told himself as he burrowed deeper into his sleeping bag. Just your imagination. Go to sleep.

The sounds continued.

But he had to ignore them. His reputation in Scout Troop 2000 was already shot. If he didn't get his act together, they might kick him out of the troop.

Then he heard a scream.

A bloodcurdling scream.

Brad's scream.

His heart pounding, Adam peeked out of his sleeping bag.

In the dim moonlight from Botania-9's two quarter moons, Adam could see Brad rising into the air—tangled in thick creeping vines that curled around him like arms!

Adam prayed he was dreaming, but he knew it was real.

Giant treelike plants had surrounded their camp—trees with eyes that blinked in the darkness! The one that had captured Brad in its twisting vines now carried him upward toward what looked like a huge gaping mouth—

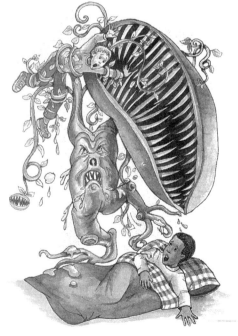

The mouth of a giant Venus's-flytrap!

Adam screamed. "Wake up! Everybody, wake up!"

"Aw, go to sleep," Zedron mumbled from his sleeping pod.

But when Halley screamed, too, Zedron and the other scouts scrambled to their feet. In the darkened confusion Adam saw that several other of the giant flytraps were drooling over the rest of them, their vines curling like snakes into their sleeping bags.

One plucked Halley from the ground and raised her skyward.

"*Aaaaaaghhh!*" she screamed.

Mr. Gordon stood there, speechless, frozen with fear.

"Quick!" Ylana cried. "We've got to do something!" She grabbed up her Swiss Army knife and ran to the plant that was trying to eat Halley. Over and over again she stabbed the knife into the base of the plant. Green stinky slime glowed as it oozed from the cuts, but the monstrous plant barely flinched.

Adam ran to help her, but suddenly a stringy vine wrapped itself tightly around his chest.

He couldn't breathe! The pressure crushed the air from his lungs. Then he felt a sharp pain near his heart—the can of insect repellent in his front pocket was stabbing into him beneath the pressure of the vine.

With his last ounce of strength, Adam tried to twist away, but only succeeded in lodging the bug spray under his chin. Adam closed his eyes as a sharp blast of poison bug spray soaked his shirt.

Suddenly the plant's grip relaxed.

Confused, Adam rolled away from the plant. His hand closed around the can of bug spray. Could that be it?

"Halley! Brad!" he shouted. "Cover your nose and mouth! Try not to breathe!"

"*Aaahhhhh!*" Brad screamed.

The scoutmaster dug out his communicator and signaled the starship *Euphoria*. "Come in, *Euphoria*. Scout Troop 2000 is in emergency mode. Need rescue immediately!"

Adam raised his canister of insect repellent and sprayed at the vines encircling Brad. They shrank back, dropping Brad like a sack of potatoes.

"Ow!" Brad yelped.

"Get back!" Adam ordered him. Then he charged the plants, firing shots of bug spray like an intergalactic ranger blasting renegade spacecraft.

The plants cowered at Adam's charge. They were retreating!

Halley tumbled to the ground.

"Are you all right?" Ylana asked as she ran to help the weeping girl.

"I'm . . . okay," she managed, then wiped her hands on her clothes. "Except for this horrible green goo!"

"Quick," Mr. Gordon ordered them. "Leave your things. Run!"

"Where?" someone cried.

"The *Euphoria* is sending a rescue vehicle for us. Follow Brad's screams."

Adam and the other scouts ran toward the broad field where Brad's tiny figure could be seen hysterically waving his tiny laserflash at a descending rescue ship.

The ship landed quickly and rescuers jumped out to hustle the kids onboard.

But as Adam glanced back over his shoulder, he saw that the giant plants had recovered and were quickly moving toward them again. Soon they'd surround the ship.

Adam shook his can of bug spray and pressed the

release valve. A pitiful *fffttt!* told him he'd used up all the spray.

Adam dropped the empty can and hurried up the ladder into the ship . . .

Horrible vines of a giant plant snaked around the door, preventing it from closing. From inside, Adam could see other vines curling over the ship through the windows.

"They're holding us down," the pilot shouted to Mr. Gordon. "If we don't get them off, we can't leave!"

Suddenly Adam had an idea. He dashed to the ship's galley and jabbed some buttons on the food replicator.

"How can you think of eating at a time like this?" Halley screeched.

But Adam was too busy to answer. Several excruciatingly long seconds later he dashed to the ship's door.

He sailed something over the heads of Ylana and Mr. Gordon.

And suddenly the monster plant gripping the door let go.

Adam fired another missile out the door. "Quick!" he shouted to the pilot. "Start the engines—but leave the door open till the last minute!"

Adam tossed four or five more missiles toward the plants just before the door slid shut and the rescue ship blasted off.

They could see vines slipping away from the windows as the plants let go.

Everyone watched silently as Botania-9 grew smaller and smaller in the viewing port.

"Free and clear," the pilot announced.

Everyone cheered.

"Hey, Adam," said a frightened Brad, peeking through his fingers as he sat curled up in the corner. "What the heck did you fire at those plants?"

Adam grinned. "Pepperoni and Italian sausage pizza," he said. "I figured the plants were hungry."

The scouts' laughter filled the ship as they headed toward the starship *Euphoria*.

MY SISTER IS A REAL BRAT!

I opened my closet door, looking for my secret stash of afternoon snack cakes and candy bars.

And screamed!

An alien leaped from the darkness and roared at me: "Die, earthling vermin!"

Then the scaly green face with its row of six eyes twisted into hysterical laughter.

Little girl laughter.

"You are such a brat!" I yelled at my little sister, Una.

She'd done it again. She'd managed to scare the living daylights out of me. My heart was pounding like a punching bag.

You'd think I'd be used to it. She loves to wear that stupid old Halloween mask and jump out at me and she always manages to catch me when I'm not expecting it.

"I'm going to tell Mom!" I snapped.

For once my bratty sister seemed really scared. "Wait—please don't!"

Mom hates that mask of hers. She doesn't like scary stuff. And she told Una if she ever caught her wearing it again, she'd be in big trouble.

"Gotcha!" I grinned like a cat.

Una glared at me. "If you tell her, I'll squeal on you about all the junk food you keep in here."

"You wouldn't!" I shouted.

"Gotcha!"

"All right, all right, I won't tell," I said angrily. "Now get out! You know you're not supposed to be in my room. Can't you read?" I pointed at the sign on my door.

**PRIVATE!!!
LITTLE SISTERS
AND OTHER ALIENS—
KEEP OUT!!**

"Hey, you're not the emperor of the universe!" Una snapped back. "I don't have to take orders from you."

I grabbed her arm and shoved her out into the hall, then slammed the door and locked it. "And stay out!"

"I hate you, you stupid flodgepit!" she shouted through the door.

I laughed in disgust. What a baby. Eight years old and still making up silly words.

Every year I make the same wish when I blow out the candles on my birthday cake: that I was an only child!

But it never comes true. So I guess I'm stuck with her.

I guess you can tell my little sister and I hate each other. We fight all the time, and it drives Mom and Dad crazy. What drives me crazy is that I usually get blamed, because my parents say I should know better since I'm in middle school.

Like tonight after supper. I was watching the basketball game on TV.

Una marched right in, snatched the remote, and switched it to the Sci-Fi Channel. Some aliens were attacking a couple of teenagers watching TV in their living room. It's the kind of movie I might have enjoyed watching. But the fact that she just changed the channel without asking me really steamed me.

"Hey, I was watching the game!" I shouted, grabbing for the remote.

"Too bad," she said. Then she sat down right in front of me. "Nanny, nanny, boo-boo."

I snatched the remote from her grubby hand and switched back to the game.

Una jumped to her feet. "You're the meanest brother in the universe—and I'm going to tell Mom and Dad!"

I was so mad at her! "Mom and Dad aren't even your real parents!" I yelled. "And I'm not your real brother. You were adopted!"

That seemed to stop her in her tracks!

But then—I couldn't believe it—she threw back her head and laughed. "You wish!"

But Mom had just walked into the family room, and she heard everything I said. For some reason, it really upset her.

"Don't you ever say anything like that again!" she told me. She fell to her knees and hugged us both, one in each arm. "Each of you is very special to me, and I love you both."

Una squirmed out of Mom's arms and fell on the floor laughing. What a lunatic.

Mom looked close to tears.

"That's enough, you two," Dad said, storming into the family room. He snapped off the TV. "Go to your rooms, both of you."

"But, Dad," I whined, "the game—"

"He started it!" Una added.

"Now!" Dad bellowed.

Una stuck out her tongue at me, and I mirrored the expression as we trudged upstairs. I hurried into my room, slammed the door, and made sure I locked it.

38

See what I mean? I'd just been minding my own business, watching the game. But she had to ruin everything and get us in trouble.

Boy, I wish she really were adopted.

But of course, she's not. And that's one of the reasons I hate her—because she's so much like Dad. She looks just like him. Sleek black hair, green eyes, not blond-haired and blue-eyed like me. And she's a little genius, just like Dad—computer whiz, top prizes at the science fair, 100s on all her math tests, stuff like that. I guess that's why Dad always spends more time with her than with me.

Well, if she wasn't adopted, and I couldn't wish her away with birthday candles, maybe she'd get lost in the woods. Or kidnapped!

I gazed out my window at the stars twinkling in the dark night. A shooting star streaked across the sky, and I made a wish.

I wished a UFO would land in our backyard and kidnap my bratty little sister!

That night I woke up suddenly. Someone was in my room!

I started to shriek, but as my eyes grew used to the dark, I realized who it was.

My sister! I could see her beady little head outlined in the faint glow from the hallway night-light. She was wearing that stupid alien mask again. Good grief. Did she sleep in the thing?

Hey! How'd she get in? I wondered. My door was locked!

I started to yell at her to get out!

But then I decided to wait and see what she was up to. Was she going to try to scare me again? Hah! Good luck!

Maybe I'd jump up and scare the pants off her for a change. It would serve her right.

I lay still, barely breathing. This was going to be great.

I felt Una stare at me a moment. But she didn't try to scare me. Instead, she went to my computer and clicked it on.

How dare she touch my computer without asking!

Then I realized she was carrying something. It was a CD-ROM disc. But not just an ordinary disc. It glowed in the dark! Where'd she get that!?

She slipped it into my computer, waited for the icon to come up on the screen, then clicked it open.

Wildly colored graphics flashed on the screen, but I couldn't read the garbled words.

I shivered. Una's mask looked really scary in the glow of the computer screen.

Almost real.

Then I noticed her hands—twisted claws that matched her scaly green mask. I choked back a gasp. When did she get those?

Una's creepy fingers flew across the keyboard for a few minutes till she heard a soft chiming signal.

Then I heard her speak, and her voice sounded older, deeper, and really weird. As if a thousand bees buzzed in her throat.

"The research is nearly finished," she informed the computer. "How much longer?"

And then someone answered her—in that same deep buzzing voice. "Soon," it said. "Be prepared to return to Sibilus at any moment. Our plans are accelerating."

Chills tiptoed down my spine. What kind of weird on-line game was this?

Una laughed softly, a deep rumbling laugh. "Excellent, commander," she said. "I cannot tolerate this disgusting Earth boy much longer."

"Forget the boy," the commander boomed. "Just

41

conclude your assignment. Then our mission will be complete."

I broke out into a cold sweat. I lay as still as I could. What's going on?

My little sister suddenly stopped and glanced sharply at me. I thought my heart would stop. Then I saw that it wasn't just her face and hands that were scaly green. So were her bare arms and legs sticking out from her ridiculous frilly pink nightgown.

Her band of six eyes glowed like little neon-green stars. And she was wearing something pointy in her hair.

No! She'd sprouted some kind of creepy antennae!

My heart began pounding as if it wanted to rip from my chest.

I always knew my sister was weird. Now I knew why.

My sister's an alien! I felt like screaming.

Don't move! I warned myself. But I needn't have worried. Because two seconds later I fainted dead away.

When I woke up the next morning, I tossed back my covers and stretched. But midstretch I remembered—and almost fainted again!

My sister's an alien!

But wait, I told myself. Calm down. Maybe you only dreamed it.

I stood up. Then I stared at the floor.

A thin trail of smelly slime led from my desk to the door.

The slimy trail of an alien!

I dressed with trembling hands. I stepped into the hall and crept toward the door to Una's room. I was almost too afraid to look inside. What would I see?

But the room was empty. The bed looked as if it had never been slept in. She must be downstairs already.

How could I face her?

How could I tell Mom and Dad without Una finding out?

I had to pretend I suspected nothing. But what if she could tell I was on to her? Would she zap me into a pile of scorched slush with her neon-green vision?

Taking a deep breath, I slowly walked downstairs to the kitchen. There they sat, the perfect American family, having breakfast like a cereal commercial.

Mom, Dad, and my little sister, the alien!

"Morning, sweetheart," my mom said. "Did you sleep well?"

"Uh, yeah," I mumbled and slid into my seat.

Una stared across the table at me, as if she were trying to read my mind. But today her eyes were just regular green, like Dad's—not glowing like neon-green stars.

She stuck her tongue out at me.

Without thinking, I returned the gesture.

Oh, great, I told myself. I just insulted an alien! What would she do? Suck my eyeballs out? Crush me between her claws with her super alien strength?

"Mom! He stuck his tongue out at me!" Una whined.

"Well, she did it first!" I shot back.

"Now, don't you two start," Dad warned from behind his newspaper. "Just ignore each other and eat your breakfast."

I dug into my Frosty Fruitios, but I could barely eat. Thinking about Una's scaly green face, her creepy claws, her trail of slime sort of ruined my appetite.

But the longer I stared at her, the more I began to wonder. She looked so normal in the bright morning sunlight that streamed in through the kitchen window. Obnoxious, yes, but normal.

Had I dreamed the whole thing?

Maybe my sister wasn't an alien. Maybe she was just a plain old brat.

I began to relax. Yeah, that was it. I hated my sister so much, I was having nightmares about her.

But then, just before she left to catch her bus, I saw her slip that glowing CD-ROM disc into her book bag.

The nightmare was true!

I stared at my cereal bowl until she was gone, icy prickles dancing down my spine.

As soon as I heard her bus pull away down the street, I tried to tell my parents. "Mom! Dad! I found out something terrible last night! My little sister's an alien!" I sputtered. "She's trying to contact aliens on another planet from my computer! She has neon-green eyes and antennae—"

Dad just ignored me from behind his newspaper.

Mom just shook her head as she put her coffee cup into the dishwasher. "You two . . ."

"But it's true!" I insisted. "She came into my room last night. I saw her! She's got green skin, and six eyes—"

Dad flung down his paper in disgust. "I'm sick and tired of you and your sister bickering all the time and trying to get each other in trouble. This sibling rivalry business has got to stop!"

His chair screeched as he stood up and muttered, "Sometimes I wish we'd never—"

"John!" Mom exclaimed. She gave him a warning look, and he stomped out of the room.

Mom gave me a quick hug. "Just ignore your father. He has a lot of important . . . business on his mind right now. He's on edge. And you and Una really upset him. Think you can be a good big brother and lay off a while?"

"But, Mom—"

"You're going to be late for school," she said firmly and marched me toward the front door. "We'll talk about this some other time."

I could hardly think at school all day. And right in the middle of math, I remembered.

The green smelly slime trail!

I should have shown Mom and Dad! I'd do it this afternoon. Then they'd *have* to believe me.

As soon as I got home, I told my mom about the green slime.

She sighed, shaking her head in exasperation.

"Come on, I'll show you!"

Just then I saw Una standing in the doorway, staring angrily at me. She'd heard!

"Show me," Mom ordered.

Trembling, I led Mom upstairs, with my sister tagging along like a pesky mosquito. What would Una do when I revealed the evidence? Would Mom be able to protect me? Or would she annihilate both of us on the spot?

When I reached my room, I flung open my door and pointed to the floor.

Then I stopped short. Except for that soda stain next to my bed, the carpet was clean. The slime trail had vanished. And so had my proof!

"I don't see anything," Mom said.

Una laughed. "Maybe you shouldn't eat Goober Bars and Debbie Doodle Cakes before bedtime," she cracked. "It's giving you nightmares."

Mom threw up her hands and left the room. Una turned to stick out her tongue.

And she glared at me with neon-green eyes sparkling like stars.

I gulped. Now I was really in trouble.

She knew I was on to her.

For the next few days I did the only thing I knew how to do. I lay low. I tried not to talk to her. I held my tongue, even when she called me names, like "meteor brain" and "scumbot."

And I watched and waited.

Waiting for some proof that I could take to my parents.

Every night now my sister came into my room to use the computer.

Every night I pretended to be sound asleep.

I heard all her plans.

Then one day my measly earthling brain erupted with a brilliant idea.

My tape recorder! Dad had given me one of those small microcassette recorders for my last birthday. It was perfect!

That night I waited for her, with my tape recorder barely hidden beneath by my sheet.

When Una came into my room, I held my breath and pressed the Record button, hoping that her antennae wouldn't pick up the tiny click.

Soon I heard the words that I will never forget. "Taking over Earth," Una said in her deep buzzing voice, "will be like taking floznyet from a baby Algronian."

Yes!

At last—I had the proof I needed.

The next morning I waited till Una left on the school bus. Then I slipped my tape recorder out of my backpack and laid it on the kitchen table.

"Mom, Dad," I said. "Listen to this."

My hands trembled as I pressed the Play button.

It was all there. Una talking in that weird voice to some commander guy in another galaxy. And then those cryptic words, spoken in that weird deep buzzing voice: "Taking over Earth will be like taking floznyet from a baby Algronian."

I pressed Stop and looked expectantly at my parents.

"Is that for a school project?" Dad asked as he put the orange juice back in the fridge.

I stared at him. "Huh?"

Mom giggled. "How did you make your voice sound like that?" She asked as she picked up her purse. "It's really cute."

"But, Mom, Dad!" I cried. "You don't understand! That wasn't me. That was Una! Talking in her alien voice! Didn't you hear—"

"John, dear," Mom said to Dad. "Could you give me a ride to the supermarket on your way to work?"

"Of course, Martha." Dad looked at his watch. "But we'd better hurry. I'm going to be late."

Mom blew me a kiss. "Don't forget to lock the door on your way out, sweetheart."

And then they were gone.

I stood there with my mouth hanging open.

They didn't believe me. They thought I'd just been fooling around with the tape recorder! I laid my head on the table. I felt like giving up.

Soon aliens would be taking over planet Earth. But how could I stop them if no one believed me?

That afternoon I peeked into the family room and saw Una do a whole page of math problems in thirty seconds flat. Then she ran outside to play. I snuck into her backpack and pulled out her work. And I found pages and pages of notes in strange alien characters. I grabbed several sheets and stuffed them into my shirt.

That night, after Una had gone to bed, I sat down at the kitchen table and showed my parents the alien writing. "You just gotta believe me, Mom and Dad. Una's an alien. And if we don't do something, she and her alien pals are going to take over the Earth."

Mom and Dad exchanged glances.

Dad sighed. "This can't go on."

"But, John—"

"Martha, it's too late. He's never going to give up." Dad glanced at me sadly. "I think it's time we told him the truth."

"Oh, please, John, can't it wait?" Mom asked.

Aha! I thought. They do know something weird is going on here! I knew it! My little sister's adopted. She's an alien. She's—She's—

Mom and Dad left the room.

The next thing I knew, they'd dragged several suitcases down the stairs and hustled me and my sister into the car.

"What's going on?" I asked nervously. "Where are we going?"

Dad didn't answer me. He just kept staring out the windshield as he drove out of our neighborhood.

Mom leaned over the front seat and gently patted my hand. "Don't worry, sweetheart. Your father and I will explain everything soon." She smiled, but her eyes

were filled with worry.

We drove on and on into the dark night, onto the highway, then off the highway, down long twisting dirt roads. Every now and then my little sister would poke me or kick me till Dad yelled at her to leave me alone. After that she spent the rest of the trip with her nose pressed against her window, staring up into the sky as if she wished she were up there with all her creepy alien friends.

She didn't wish it more than I did.

I might have fallen asleep if I hadn't been so scared. Maybe I dozed, I don't know. The night was so dark and silent.

Finally I felt the car jostling as Dad drove off the dirt road straight across a field hidden by a ring of trees. At last he parked the car and shut off the motor.

The night was silent except for the chirp of crickets. I figured we must be far from the city, because the constellations shone brighter in the sky than I'd ever seen them.

Dad and Una jumped out of the car without a word.

Mom got out and came around to my door. "Come, sweetheart," she crooned, holding out her hand. "Do not be afraid."

I clutched my mother's hand. It made me feel warm and safe. But somehow her words only frightened me more.

A few yards away an old abandoned barn stood in the moonlight, its blood-red paint peeling away like dead skin.

Mom slipped her arm around my shoulder. The barn doors moaned as Dad pulled them open.

Something was in there. It was hard to see in the dark. Some kind of big vehicle or machine or something.

Impatiently Dad waved us all inside, and then he closed the barn doors, dropping the wooden latch in place.

Then Dad held up his hand and slowly rotated it clockwise in front of a small glowing red rectangle on the side of the vehicle.

A door whooshed open, and a shaft of golden light fell around my feet.

My parents quickly hustled me inside.

I couldn't believe what I saw.

High-tech computer equipment blinked and hummed around a circular console. It looked like a spaceship—or a UFO! Was this some kind of secret project Dad was working on?

"Dad! What is this—"

And then I heard the door slam shut.

I jumped.

My dad started to explain. But Mom raised her hand. "John, please. Let me." She laid her hands on my shoulders. She had a smile on her face, but her eyes

filled with tears. "You see, sweetheart, your little sister isn't adopted."

"Sh-she's not?"

"No," Mom said. She took a deep breath, then said softly, "You are."

"I am?" I cried.

Whoa! I was totally blown away. I would never have expected that in a million years.

Mom nodded. "It's true. And you were right. Una is an—ahem—'alien,' as you put it. She comes from the planet Sibilus."

"I guess I don't have to wear this anymore," Una said. She reached up and yanked off her face as if it were a mask—it was a mask!—revealing her true features beneath.

That green face with the band of six neon-green eyes.

I shrieked. I had known it, tried to prove it, and yet, somehow I had wanted to hear my mother deny it, explain it away, the way she had often soothed away my nightmares. To hear her admit that it was true made it seem even more terrifying. "Mom, Dad! Quick! Call 911! The FBI! The Marines! The—the—"

Then it struck me.

My sister was not adopted. And my sister was an alien. That must mean . . .

Mom and Dad stared at me with a look of pity in their eyes. Eyes that glowed neon-green like sparkling

stars.

My mom and dad were aliens, too!

I stared, my mouth hanging open. I couldn't speak. My feet felt glued to the floor.

The two people I loved most in the world, the people who had raised me from birth, the people I had trusted to keep me safe from all the horrors and nightmares in the world . . .were aliens from another planet.

Mom reached for me, but I took a step back.

Her face twisted in agony. So Dad continued.

"We're scientists. We came to Earth to do advanced research for the approaching invasion. We've been here a long time, since just before you were born, for there has been a great deal of work to do. You were adopted to add to our cover. You gave us the chance to observe human beings up close and to add reality to our impersonations. And we had noticed from monitoring your television that the perfect family seemed to have two children, the oldest one a boy."

Una made a rude noise, and Dad glared at her.

Mom wiped a tear from her eye. "The only complication was—I never realized how much I'd come to love you." She wrapped her arms around me in a great big hug.

Somehow it didn't feel the same anymore.

My sister snorted in disgust.

My dad—or whoever he was—shook his head impatiently. "Now, Martha, none of that." Then he continued his story. "Our planet is dying, and we need a new one to colonize. We've acquired all the necessary data, and now we're heading home. Our report will help our leaders decide whether to eradicate all earthlings—or just make them slaves."

I couldn't believe how coldly this man I had called Dad spoke of killing people. People like me.

"Do we have to take him with us?" Una whined.

"Of course!" Mom exclaimed. "He's—he's like a son to me."

Dad shrugged. "She made me promise, Una. It's a glitch in the plans, but we'll deal with it. Besides," he added, turning his cold eyes on me, "he knows too much to leave behind."

"Aw, plitzfiz!" Una pouted and glared at me, her neon-green eyes glowing like tiny stars.

Suddenly I could move, and I ran to the door. But there was no handle, no knob. I clutched at the edges, pounded frantically on the cold smooth metal.

No way out.

My mom—or *whatever* she was—grabbed my shoulders and sat me down on a cushioned seat built into the wall. Gently but firmly, she strapped me in with a seat-beltlike harness. Then she brought me something warm to drink. It was purple and tasted the way gasoline smells.

Dad's fingers flew across the panel of blinking keys, and I felt the spaceship rumble to life. Then he, Mom,

and Una strapped themselves into seats as well.

Una glared at me with pure hatred in her eyes.

What would become of me? It was too horrifying to imagine. But as we blasted off toward the stars, I couldn't help but think:

I wish I'd been nicer to my little sister.

HOME SWEET HOME

Andromeda woke up startled and banged her head on the top of her sleeping tube.

Someone was in her room compartment.

Her night-light sensed her upright position and increased its glow by twenty watts.

"Grandma . . . ?"

"Shhh," her grandmother whispered. "Come. I

have something to show you. Something important."

Andromeda shoved her long strawberry blond hair out of her face and yawned. Feeling beside her, she pressed the oval button beside her night-light and her alarm clock announced: "The time is . . . two forty-seven."

"Grandma!" Andromeda exclaimed. "It's the middle of the night!"

Grandma Rose just smiled. "It's a good time for confidences."

Andromeda leaned back on her pillow and stared at her grandmother. She was tall and slender and had a beautiful head of white hair that she wore in an old-fashioned style on top of her head. Her face was lined, but her eyes still sparkled with energy.

Andromeda loved her, but . . . people said she was a crazy old lady. Always talking about things that didn't make sense, always talking about the past . . . when people still lived on Earth.

Grandma Rose even insisted on making her tea by boiling water when the food replicator was so quick and easy and not messy at all.

Andromeda loved her grandmother, but sometimes it was embarrassing when everybody called your grandmother a moonloony. Luckily, the old woman spent most of her time down in the Senior Center, playing odd games with other old people. Andromeda felt sorry for them, they seemed so out of touch with real life in Earth II.

Long before Andromeda was born, when Grandma

Rose was just a young married girl, Earth became so polluted and torn apart by wars that a few hundred people blasted off to start an experimental colony on Mars. Everyone hoped that one day they could return to Earth. But if not, they would continue to survive in the Earth II colony.

Over the decades, Andromeda had learned in school, their scientists and engineers had built onto that first small colony and turned it into a remarkable structure that met all their needs. Astronauts made short forays to the Outside for raw materials, but otherwise no one ever left. Generations passed, and the governing council reported that civilization on Earth had destroyed itself. They would never be able to return.

Andromeda didn't see what the big deal was. She loved Earth II. They lived a life of peace, luxury, and safety. They manufactured their atmosphere, their food, their energy. Everyone had clean, comfortable living compartments. A giant-screen TV in each home educated them, entertained them, governed them, kept them informed. Andromeda was happy. They had everything they needed. Why long for some dead world from the past?

"Come now," Grandma Rose insisted. "Let's go wake your brother."

Andromeda slipped out of her sleeping tube. "Okay. But he's not gonna like this."

She followed her grandmother into the compartment next to hers. Grandma Rose gave the tangled

lump in the sleeping tube a gentle shake. "Orion—Orion, wake up!"

A blond head appeared for a moment. "What time is it?" Orion mumbled. He buried his head under his pillow and waved them away.

But Grandma Rose wouldn't be put off. "Come, grandson! Up and at 'em! I'm not sure how much time I have left," she said with a chuckle, though her eyes looked sad. "There are things I want to show you two. Things someone in our family must know."

Andromeda yanked the covers off her brother. "Come on!" Her eyes shone with excitement now that she was fully awake. "I want to see Grandma's secret!"

"All right, all right. I'm coming," he said.

Andromeda and Orion followed their grandmother, tiptoeing down the narrow corridor of their family's apartment. She ushered them into her room, then closed the door and locked it. A small light glowed by her bed. Beside it sat a large rectangular object.

Orion immediately ran his hand over the brown surface. "Grandma!" he exclaimed. "What is this?"

"It's a box." Grandma Rose chuckled. "Made of wood."

Andromeda gasped. "You mean like from trees?"

They had read that long ago homes and many other things on Earth had been made from wood. But inside Earth II they had few trees and they were so small and slender that no one would dream of cutting them down.

"This used to belong to my great-grandmother Marcella," Grandma Rose went on.

"What's it for?" Andromeda asked.

"In here I keep my mementos from Earth," she explained.

Orion's eyes shot up. "But isn't that—"

"Yes, yes, my child, it's illegal." Grandma Rose shook her head. "When we first came to live here, the governing council took away most Earth possessions to use as raw materials. And I, like the others, gladly gave up most things to contribute to our survival. Other things were destroyed for fear they might be contaminated with viruses, bacteria, or pollutants that would harm the colony. It was for the good and the safety of everyone."

"We read about that in school," Orion said.

"But some of these things—I simply could not part with them," Grandma Rose said as she opened the large wooden lid.

Eyes shining, she pulled out an object.

Andromeda reached for it, but Orion grabbed her hand. "Don't! These things could be dangerous!"

"Hogwash!" Grandma Rose admonished. "Nothing in here would hurt a fly. They're just ordinary things from Earth."

But to Andromeda they did not seem ordinary at all. The trunk was filled with strange things, things she'd seen only in pictures on the computer.

A dried flower so unlike the ones they grew in the colony greenhouse. It still smelled sweet yet—"Ouch!" She pricked her finger on the odd spikes that lined the stem. They didn't have flowers that pricked in Earth II.

"It's a rose—with thorns," Grandma Rose explained. "The one your grandfather gave me on our first date. 'A rose for a Rose,' he said."

Orion was curious about an odd curled object the size of his hand.

"A shell," Grandma Rose said, then added with a grin, "If you hold it up to your ear, you can hear the ocean."

Orion held the shell to his ear and smiled at the odd whistling sound. "What's an ocean?"

Grandma Rose tried to explain. "It's a huge body of water on Earth—larger than Earth II itself. It's filled with strange and wonderful sea creatures. And it can be peaceful and calm one moment, stormy and dangerous the next."

Andromeda grabbed the shell from her brother and listened. "It sounds lonesome to me."

It was hard to understand this ocean Grandma Rose described. Water was so precious in Earth II.

"And this." Grandma Rose held up an old plastic jar with the strange word *Jif* printed on a faded label. It was filled with some kind of black material. "Dirt! Good old earth. We used to grow food in it."

Andromeda wrinkled up her nose. "Unreal!" She had never eaten anything that wasn't grown by hydro-ponics—farming done completely in nutrient solutions.

Next she held up what looked to Andromeda like more dirt, but lighter in color. Grandma Rose sprinkled some into her hand. "Sand. From the shores of the Atlantic Ocean."

Then Grandma Rose pulled from her trunk the strangest things of all—different-colored rectangles, each about the size of a small computer. Each was filled with pale sheets of a musty-smelling fragile material.

"Books," she told them.

"What are they for?" Andromeda asked. She opened one and saw that the pages were covered with words applied to the sheets in some permanent way. A few pages even had colored pictures.

"You read them."

"What?" Orion scoffed. He and Andromeda read and wrote on the computer. They had heard of paper, but neither had ever seen any.

Orion rubbed his fingers across the pages. "What good are stories and news without moving pictures and sounds? What good are pages where the words can't be deleted or changed? And look how much space one story takes up."

Grandma Rose pressed a book into each child's hand. To Orion she gave *The Adventures of Huckleberry Finn*, by Mark Twain. To Andromeda, *Little Women*, by Louisa May Alcott. "Read them," Grandma Rose insisted. "Then tell me what you think. But keep the books hidden. Your parents might not understand."

Grandma Rose's old-fashioned clock chimed the hour. She had been able to keep the strange timepiece since no one else had any use for a clock where you had to calculate the time by measuring a short hand and minute hand.

"It is late," Grandma Rose said. "I have more to tell you. But perhaps we should take it a little at a time. Back to bed with you both."

Orion took his book reluctantly, but Andromeda hugged hers to her chest. "Can we come back again later? And look at your things some more?"

Grandma Rose smiled in delight. "Of course, child. Soon. Very soon."

The next morning Andromeda grinned across the breakfast table at Orion. He rolled his eyes.

Dad was reading the electronic news output on a small handheld TV screen. Their mother was updating a report on her laptop computer.

"Did you read your book?" Andromeda whispered.

"Shhh!" Orion hissed, glancing at his parents. "And no—I don't have time for silly time wasters like that."

"Oh, Orion, you must!" she whispered. She told him how she had read hers the night before. The experience was strange—to read something with no electrical connection to others, curled up in her sleeping cell, without the hum and glare of a computer screen. It was so private, almost secretive. And the story, about life on Earth more than three hundred years ago, was exciting.

"Sounds stupid to me," Orion mumbled. But at last he promised he would try.

Andromeda didn't see much of her grandmother for the next few days. She was always down at the Senior Center, her head bent over something, whispering with some of the other old people as if they had a secret.

A few nights later Grandma Rose came to them again in the night. Her old face was glowing, her eyes shining. To her grandchildren, she seemed happier than they'd ever seen her.

"Grandma Rose, what is it?" Andromeda asked. "What's happened?"

"I need your help," she whispered excitedly. "I'm going to escape."

"Escape?" Andromeda gasped. The word made no sense to her. "Escape from what? To where?"

"I want to escape from Earth II," she announced. "To the Outside."

"Are you crazy!" Orion yelped.

"Shhh!" Grandma Rose warned.

"You're crazy," Orion said. "You'll die on the Outside."

Grandma Rose stubbornly shook her head. "I'm going, and that's final."

"Well, you can't," Orion said. "We won't let you. And besides, we wouldn't even know how to get out."

Grandma Rose grinned and unfolded a small crumpled piece of paper. A crudely drawn map of lines and twists and turns curled across the sheet.

"What crackpot down at the Senior Center sold you that?" Orion asked.

But Grandma Rose paid him no mind. "I'm going whether you help me or not. But I want to take my trunk. And I could use some help carrying that."

"Oh, brother!" Orion said.

But Andromeda took him aside. "Listen, Orion.

She's really going to do this! Let's pretend to go along with her so we can find out what's going on."

"And then what?" he demanded.

"I don't know," Andromeda replied. "You're the smart one, big brother. I'm sure you'll think of some way to stop her."

Fifteen minutes later the three stepped out into the dark corridor. Andromeda had never been outside her family's apartment this late at night. The night shifts would be up and running on the other side of the colony, but here the corridors were dark and quiet.

Suddenly they heard footsteps up ahead.

"Get down," Orion whispered.

But Grandma Rose kept walking. "Come on!"

A white-haired night patrolman stepped out of the shadows. "Well, well, well, what do we have here?" he asked.

"Good evening, Jeremiah," Grandma Rose said without even blinking.

"Nice night for a moonlit walk, eh?" Jeremiah asked.

Grandma Rose chuckled, then added, "Take care, Jeremiah. Come see us sometime."

The night watchman grinned. "Well, now, I might just do that one of these days." Then he strolled on down the hall, whistling softly.

Orion and Andromeda couldn't believe it. He hadn't stopped them. He hadn't reported them!

"Come on, you two," Grandma Rose whispered urgently.

Soon they were on Level Q. Orion stopped and stared out the viewport at the beautiful black sky dotted with stars, the tiny glowing Earth in the distance. "What could be more beautiful?" he asked softly. Then he frowned at his grandmother. "And why would anybody in their right mind want to leave?"

The map led them down, down, past most living quarters into the lower levels of Earth II. Neither of the kids had ever been so far from their apartment. Now all they saw were pipes and wiring and storage, the forgotten bowels of the colony.

Suddenly up ahead they saw a light blink on and off.

"Grandma, look!" Andromeda whispered.

Orion tried to stop her, but Grandma Rose ran ahead like an eager young girl.

An old man was signaling them. "Ah," he said. "And the young ones are going, too?" he asked, eyebrows raised, but smiling.

"How could I leave behind what I love most?" Grandma Rose asked, and the old man nodded.

The man moved aside some crates, pressed a small black mark on the wall, and a trapdoor slid open in the floor.

Grandma zipped up her jumpsuit and started down the stairs. "Thanks, Roberto. I owe you one."

Andromeda followed, and Roberto helped Orion carry the huge trunk down the stairs.

The stairs led to what looked like an abandoned subway platform. And resting in the tunnel was a small old-fashioned rocket ship.

"It looks like a toy ride from the arcade!" Orion scoffed.

"Come!" Grandma Rose ordered as she climbed through the door of the ship.

"Grandma, no!" Andromeda gasped.

"Are you crazy?" Orion exclaimed. He turned on Roberto. "How can you let her do this?"

The old man just laughed. "Because she is my friend." He loaded the trunk into a cargo bay, then waved through the door at their grandmother. "Good luck!"

Angry now, Orion strode into the ship, with Andromeda right behind him. "Come on, now, Grandma. This has gone far enough."

Rose slammed the door shut and locked it. Then she strapped herself into the pilot's seat and pushed some controls.

Andromeda and Orion felt the engines roar to life.

"Better buckle up," their grandmother said with a wild giggle. "Don't worry," she added over the roar. "It will be all right. You'll see. I promise!"

Orion and Andromeda quickly hooked themselves into the old-fashioned harnesses.

Orion shook his head. "She's lost her mind."

Seconds later they felt the vehicle blast off! Grandma Rose steered into total darkness, twisting and turning at breakneck speed, a roller-coaster ride charged occasionally with the flash of strobe lights.

The kids hung on for dear life, and then the ship shot out into the dark night, and they realized they

were flying outside the only world they'd ever known.

They streaked across the surface, flying low near the ground, perhaps beneath the colony's radar, for they noticed that no alarms sounded. They seemed to travel unnoticed.

"Look!" Grandma Rose said, her voice choking with emotion.

Orion and Andromeda were stunned. In the soft moonlight they saw that they were flying across a beautiful landscape, covered with lush trees and lakes and streams, like pictures from Grandma Rose's books and like the photos in their computer history books.

"But—I thought Mars was nothing but dry barren rock!" Andromeda exclaimed.

"It is," Orion said. "Something weird is going on here."

Above them the night sky was spangled with stars, and a round white moon lighted their way.

Orion nervously scanned the sky. "Where's Earth? It's not where it's supposed to be."

"Be patient," Grandma Rose said. "I'll show you."

An hour or two later Grandma Rose told them to look back over their shoulders.

They did.

And they saw Earth II, a huge bubble, rising from the ground like a giant fortress. But the oddest thing was, there were no windows or viewports.

"But that doesn't make sense," Orion said. "Just before we left, I gazed out a viewport and saw Earth and the stars in the sky!"

The dome grew smaller and smaller. In another hour or two Earth II completely disappeared.

Orion's heart sank. "Now we'll never get back."

At last Grandma Rose landed the flying contraption on some kind of crude landing strip, half hidden by scrubby pines.

"How'd she learn to fly a thing like this?" Orion whispered to his sister.

"I have a feeling there's a lot about Grandma Rose we don't know," Andromeda answered.

Grandma Rose pushed a button on the dashboard and a door slid open.

"But wait!" Orion cried. "What about oxygen?"

Grandma Rose just laughed as she climbed down from the rocket.

Orion and Andromeda were terrified as they followed her down to the ground.

"Hey—I can breathe!" Orion exclaimed.

"The air smells wonderful!" Andromeda added.

Grandma Rose chuckled.

Then the kids spotted some people rushing toward them in the moonlight. Orion stepped protectively in front of his sister and grandmother.

"Oh, don't be silly," his grandmother chided as she stepped forward to greet their welcoming party.

There were several old men and women. A couple with a baby. Twin guys about twenty. And a young girl who eyed them shyly.

Orion and Andromeda were stunned.

"Martians?" Orion asked.

"They look just like us, Grandma," Andromeda said. "Like humans."

"They are," Grandma Rose said softly. "Others who have escaped from Earth II."

Orion and Andromeda could not believe it.

"But I've never heard of anyone escaping before," Orion said.

Grandma Rose's eyebrows shot up. "Do you think they'd put it on TV?"

The small crowd welcomed them warmly. "Come," said a man Grandma Rose called Moses. "We have prepared a meal to welcome you."

But Grandma Rose told them she wanted to show her grandchildren something first. "It cannot wait."

She led them on a small hike, down a road covered with the light-colored sand, just like the sand she'd had in the jar in her trunk. Only here it was everywhere. And then the land rose into dunes of the sand, covered with tall grasses waving in a stiff salty-smelling breeze.

Grandma Rose scrambled up the steep sandy dune—and they saw an incredible vision.

A huge body of water crashing in waves upon a sandy shore.

"The ocean," Grandma Rose said softly.

Andromeda gasped in delight. "It's beautiful. What is this place, Grandma? Where are we?"

Grandma Rose smiled and sat down with them on the sand. She picked up a stick and wrote in the sand:
HOME SWEET HOME.

"Earth," she said.

Andromeda and Orion stared at her in confusion.

"They lied to us," she explained gently. "I knew it all along. And so did your grandfather. We just didn't have any proof."

"Who?" Orion demanded. "Lied about what?"

Grandma Rose explained. "When our ship of colonists first left, Earth was polluted, disease was rampant, and the planet was on the verge on self-destruction. The final great war took place, and virtually all life was destroyed. There were no known human survivors.

"But our shuttle had problems and was unable to travel to Mars. So it eventually returned to Earth. But our leaders kept it a secret from the people, to avoid a panic, for indeed the Earth—the Outside—was still too poisonous for humans to live in. So they fabricated a lie—a 'manipulated reality,' they would call it, for our safety and protection—that we were on Mars and must build a colony.

"But in the generations that followed, with most of humankind gone, the Earth began to heal itself. Now it is the paradise it once was. But the government prefers to continue the manipulated reality—because now life is all organized into one nice easy package—a single gigantic building that's easy to manage. Wars and crime are not allowed. Disease, pollution, food production, personal relationships, our thoughts and beliefs—all are easy to manage—and control. The people have become accustomed to it, and no longer question anything. The only thing missing is nature—and freedom.

"Welcome home, my sweet children," Grandma Rose whispered. "Welcome home to planet Earth."

The kids were stunned.

"It can't be true!" Orion cried.

"It is true," Grandma Rose said firmly.

"But what about the viewports?" Orion demanded. "I saw Earth—up in space—just before we left Earth II!"

"Fake," Grandma Rose said. "There are no viewports on Earth II—only continuous videos of what you would see if you were on Mars."

"But what about Mother and Father?" Andromeda asked.

Grandma Rose sighed. "They're so stubborn. . . ."

She shook her head. "They were little children when we left Earth. But something happened to them growing up in the colony. They forgot. I have spoken to them, but they refuse to believe me." She wiped away a tear. "In time I hope we can bring them here, too."

She stood and brushed the sand from her jumpsuit. "And now, my beloved children, it is time for you to decide. I am old and will not live forever. But my love for you is so strong, I wanted to share this with you. To let you decide for yourself—what will you choose?"

Orion and Andromeda stood on the shore, sand beneath their feet, salt air in their faces, the ocean gleaming with the light of a pure white moon.

Which was better? A safe clean world free of crime and war, with all their needs provided?

Or freedom—and a wilderness where anything could happen?

Andromeda rushed into her grandmother's arms.

Orion stood on the shore, trying to decide.

FREAKS

I have always hated carnivals.

Especially the sideshows. You know, where they have all these weird creatures and mutants on display for the delight of paying customers. Something about seeing other living things in captivity makes me feel sick.

But when Bizym and Bartok's 2525 Intergalactic Sideshow and Carnival came to town, my parents announced we were going.

"Can't I stay home?" I begged. "I hate carnivals."

"Of course not," Mom said. "It's our weekly family outing." Mom is big on having at least one official family outing a week.

"Besides, it should be very educational," my father said—as usual. Both my parents are top-level scientists. They have a way of looking at the world as if everything should be examined under a microscope and studied and analyzed.

They always tell me I am far too emotional about things. "You'll never make a good scientist if you let your heart get in the way of your head," my father always says. He never even considers the idea that I might not want to be a scientist.

I sighed. But I agreed to go to Bizym and Bartok's 2525 Intergalactic Sideshow and Carnival. I try to be an obedient child.

The day the carnival opened, I checked my personal pocket computer for the weather update. Maybe it would rain and we wouldn't have to go.

"Hello there, this is Wendy Beryllium with your intergalactic weather update. First, on planet Yterian—" I hit *Pause* and keyed in a request for local weather only.

"In response to overwhelming public request," Wendy reported, "the weather manipulators have provided a bright sunny day today—and every day this week. Absolutely no rain will be released until after the show closes each day. And now for the long-term report—"

I shut down my computer and went to my closet. I

chose a long mirrored dress to reflect solar rays and a matching large-brimmed hat. I have sensitive skin that burns easily on sunny days, so I have to be careful.

The carnival was already crowded by the time my family arrived. It had rides, an intergalactic food court, an invention hall, and many other attractions. I wanted to go see the art exhibit, because I had read on my pocket computer that morning that they were showing a rare Jonvian sculpture from the Hyperion galaxy.

But of course, the first thing my little brother had to see were the sideshow creatures.

"But, Father," I said. "Do I have to go, too? I hate—"

"Now, now, Shana, let's not be negative," Mother said.

"Couldn't I go to the art show while you go to the sideshow?" I asked.

"It's much more logical for us to stay together," Father said. "We'll get around to everything before the day is through."

Yeah, right, I thought. Everything my brother wants to see.

"Come on," my brother said, tugging my mother's arm. "Before it gets crowded and we have to stand in line all day."

Reluctantly I followed my family toward the long bubble dome that housed the exhibit.

A sign by the entrance said:

WARNING!

The creatures in this exhibit have been captured from many strange and fascinating planets in our galaxy—and beyond—at great risk and expense.

Many are very dangerous!
Do not feed the creatures!
Avoid putting face or hands too near the cages!

The management absolves itself of all responsibility of accidental injury.

—*Bizym and Bartok*

"Cool!" my brother exclaimed.

"Maybe we shouldn't go in!" I said.

"Aw, they're just trying to scare us to make it more fun," my brother said. "Come on!" And he dashed ahead. My parents and I hurried to catch up.

At first, I tried not to look at all, but it was impossible. The creatures were making outrageous sounds. Some clawed or fought at their cages.

What is it about our nature that makes us want to look at horrible things? I do not know. But I found myself peeking in spite of myself.

Each creature was more frightening than the next— weird mutant-looking creatures who looked nothing

like any of the people or animals that I had ever seen.

"Ewww, look at that one!" my brother cried loudly. "It's so gross! And it stinks like garbage!"

I winced. I doubted any of these creatures could understand my brother's words. But his meaning would have been clear to the dumbest animal.

And then we saw a creature more horrifying than any of the others. "Number thirty-two," I read. "Young male of the species." From a planet I'd never heard of. "Especially bloodthirsty and violent," the sign said.

The creature looked me straight in the eye.

At first I thought I'd faint.

But then I thought I glimpsed a ray of intelligence behind those strange blue-colored eyes.

I couldn't help myself. I smiled kindly at him. And—surely it was my imagination—but a look of surprise seemed to cross the creature's face.

"This is boring," my brother suddenly decided. "I'm hungry. Can we go to the food court?"

That was just like him. He never stayed interested in anything for very long.

"I want to go on the rides, too!" he cried.

He dragged us outside. I blinked in the bright sunlight as we headed for a food stand. I ordered the vegetarian plate, while my brother and parents consumed something fried.

Then it was on to the rides.

"Mother," I said, pulling her aside. "I-I suddenly don't feel well. My stomach—do you think I could skip the rides? Please?"

My mother felt my forehead and looked into my eyes. She shook her head. "Probably that weird vegetarian food you eat." She sighed and glanced at her watch. "I guess it would be all right. Meet us by the entrance in about an hour, all right?"

I agreed. I hurried to the art exhibit, but the line was so long, I decided to try it again later.

Before I realized where I was going, I had wandered back through the crowds to the sideshow.

I stepped into the cool dark interior and slowly made my way around to Number 32.

Suddenly, out of the corner of my eye, I thought I saw the alien signal me!

I turned my face away. Was it my imagination?

Then I looked at him out of the corner of my eye. He was disgusting. So horribly ugly. Could this creature be intelligent enough to communicate?

"Pssst!" the creature called. He waved me over with his oddly shaped hand.

I tried not to stand too close. The sign at the entrance had warned us of the danger.

But I couldn't help it. I was curious.

I crept up near the light-beam fencing that marked where visitors should stop. The smell was overpowering. Didn't they ever clean these cages?

"Hello," the creature whispered.

I jumped back in surprise. A shudder of fear swept over me. Amazing! He could talk! I had no idea these creatures had the intelligence to learn a language.

Not my language, of course. But Intergalactica, the

neutral, official language of space that the Intergalactic Committee of the United Nations had created forty years ago to enable people from many different planets to communicate. Since my parents were scientists, they used it almost daily in their work. I had been fluent in Intergalactica since I was four.

My curiosity overcame my fear. After glancing around, I spoke to the creature in the cage. "You—you can talk!"

"So can you," he responded quickly. "Amazing, isn't it, what we freaks can learn to do?"

Embarrassed, I tried to apologize. "I'm sorry, but—"

"Don't worry about it," the creature said. Then he added, "You've got to help me!"

"Help you? How?"

"You've got to help me escape!"

I shook my head. "Oh no. I couldn't!"

"But it's horrible in here!" the creature cried. "They keep me chained up. They're cruel to me. I can't stand the food. And I miss my family. I haven't seen them in almost a year. I've got to get home."

"Your family?" I blinked. "You have a family?"

The creature snorted in disgust. "Well, of course I do! What do you think I am? A bug or something?"

Again I blushed.

"Will you help me?" he begged.

I wish he had not chosen to speak to me. I *am* the odd one in my family. Father chides me about it often. I have such a soft heart. I thought of what my parents would say if I got caught.

"I'm sorry," I said quickly. "I can't help you." I turned to go.

The alien reached through the cage and grabbed my wrist.

The texture of his skin against mine felt strange.

"Help me—please," he begged.

The alien looked so sad. So pitiful.

I imagined what it would be like to be a prisoner on a distant planet, caged and put on display. How horrible!

I couldn't help myself. With trembling hands, I reached up and released the locking mechanism.

And immediately the alien jumped out and wrapped his creepy arm unit around my throat!

I thought I'd faint. How could I have been so foolish! "Don't move," he ordered. "And don't scream, either."

It was horrifying. Up close, Number 32's odor was overpowering—unlike anything I had ever smelled. His body felt strangely warm, almost feverish against my cool skin.

Will he hurt me? I thought frantically. Kill me? Eat me alive?

"Help me escape," he hissed into my ear, "and I might just let you go . . . unharmed."

My father was right. Just look at the fix my kind heart had gotten me into this time.

Could I trust him? It hardly mattered. I was too frightened to test him, too terrified to cry out. I didn't know what powers this creature had—how it could hurt me.

"I'll do my best," I whispered. "But we're bound to be caught. There are too many people!"

He looked around nervously.

"Give me your belt," he demanded.

"My—my belt?"

"Give it to me!"

My hands shook as I took off my new Arcadian plasticine belt.

I was astonished by what the alien did next. He wrapped one end around his neck. Then he handed me the other end.

"Pretend to be walking me home from the butcher's," he said. "I'll tell you which way to go."

"But—"

"Believe it or not, I'm considered quite a delicacy on your planet!"

Clever idea, I thought. But the thought of eating him—eeew! I'm the only one in my family who's a vegetarian. Most people these days are big meat eaters, since research scientists discovered a way to make it fat free in 2497. But not me. Somehow I could never eat anything with feelings.

The alien began to walk beside me. It looked as if he were under my control. But it was he who led the way.

"If anyone gives us any trouble," he told me, "say you're walking me home to your mom so she can prepare your birthday dinner. That should check out with just about anybody."

"Will it work?" I gasped.

"It better," he said crossly. Then he stared at me a moment. "And try not to look so scared. It's your birthday, remember?"

"I'll try," I said softly.

I held my breath as we exited the carnival grounds. The crowds were so thick, I expected someone to grab me at any moment and turn me in. But we managed to escape unwanted attention.

Instead of going home, we traveled by subway toward the outer ring of the city's complex transportation levels.

Everything went fine until we got off in Sector Yy to transfer to another train. There we were spotted by a gang of Bandals—thugs who posed as street musi-

cians to rob defenseless tourists. They knew Number 32 would fetch a good price as someone's holiday dinner. As we passed, they stopped playing and quickly cased up their instruments.

"Hurry!" I whispered. We quickened our pace, but they had no trouble trailing us through the crowd, thanks to Number 32's uniquely recognizable head. "Here!" I said, stuffing my wide-brimmed hat over his head. Guiding him so he wouldn't stumble, we managed to lose the Bandals.

The trip was a frightening adventure for me, but after a while, I felt my fear of the alien begin to subside.

At last we traveled Skyway 471 to a public spaceport.

"But what good will this do?" I asked Number 32. "What will you do?"

"From here I'll try to stow away on a cargo ship—"

At my astonished look he said, "I heard about it from some carnival workers. If I'm lucky, that will get me to an intergalactic free trade zone station. From there I hope to catch a ride on a ship of beings more friendly to my planet and race than yours."

Again, I felt as if I should apologize.

But finally it was time to say good-bye.

"Look," Number 32 said. "I'm sorry I scared you. I'm sorry I had to use you to escape. It was rotten of me. But there was no other way. I promise—I never would have hurt you."

"That's OK," I said softly. "I might have done the same thing in your position."

"You are not like all the others here," he said softly. He squeezed my hand. "I'll think of you often."

The odd creature turned to go.

"Wait!" I said.

He turned back toward me, a question in his eyes.

I held up my instant wrist videosnap Father had given me for my birthday. "May I take your picture?" I asked. "So I have something to remember your face."

And then the alien did something strange. At first I didn't know what it was. Most people wouldn't have recognized his expression. But somehow I knew it was Number 32's version of a smile.

I snapped his picture twice.

Then he dug into a pocket of his strange clothing. "Here. This is for you. I've been saving it," he said. "It's my last one. But I guess if I ever make it home, I can get plenty more."

He laid a strange object in the palm of my hand. It was a small, flat, rectangular object wrapped up like a present. I had never seen anything like it.

And when he explained to me what to do with it, my eyes popped wide open and I laughed. "You're kidding!"

The alien laughed. "You'll love it. I promise." Then he typed his name and address into my pocket computer using Intergalactica symbols. "If you're ever in my neighborhood," he said with a grin, "look me up."

"I will," I promised.

It was time for him to leave. I walked the alien to Dock L67.4002, still pretending he was groceries. A policebot slowed as it passed us, its eyebeam visor pulsing, scanning me, and I broke out into a cold sweat.

But the policebot rolled on by. Whew!

The loading bay was crowded with people from all over the universe crowding on.

"But how will you get on?" I worried. "You don't have a transport ID—or even a ticket!"

"Don't worry," he said. "I've done this before."

Suddenly the alien hugged me with his strange arm units. "Thanks," he whispered. "I'll never forget you."

And then he was gone.

I watched until Number 32 disappeared into the crowd. How would I know if he made it? Maybe he'd send me a postcard, I thought with a smile. Probably I'd never know.

I hurried up to the crowded observation deck and

watched as the cargo shuttle blasted off toward distant worlds. "Good-bye," I whispered.

Then I noticed the time readout over the information desk.

It was late! My parents would be frantic!

I ran to the subway. At the stop nearest my apartment complex, I jumped out and ran toward home. I tried to sneak in through the back door, but my parents had programmed the security system to announce my arrival.

ATTENTION! ATTENTION! DAUGHTER HAS ARRIVED VIA THE REAR ENTRANCE. ATTENTION! ATTENTION . . .

Of course, my parents yelled at me for wandering away from the carnival. And my brother made faces at me.

And then my parents sent me to my room.

Which is what I wanted, anyway.

Locked away in my room, I sat down on my bed and pulled the alien's present from my pocket.

I ripped off the wrapping with the strange lettering and stared at the long pink rectangle in the palm of my hand, my heart pounding.

Then I quickly popped it into my mouth and chewed.

How sweet it was!

And after about six tries, I managed to blow a bubble—*Pop!* Just as the alien, Roger Johnson, from Oklahoma, planet Earth, had told me to do.

I gazed at my videosnap of the alien, with his weird red hair and face that had odd brownish-red spots all over it. He had two blue eyes, instead of one like me. He stood upright on two legs, instead of five. His skin was smooth and pale, so different from my thick aqua slime covering. No antennae grew out of the top of his head and his two arm units looked nothing like my four long tentacles.

Yes, the alien was still quite ugly, but somehow, in my heart, I knew I would never look at aliens quite the same way again.

DISNEY PRESS UNLEASHES ITS LIVE-ACTION BOOKS

GET A FREE ISSUE OF

The fun-filled magazine that kids enjoy and parents applaud.

A whopping one million kids ages 7 to 14 are dedicated to reading Disney Adventures—you will be, too!

Each month DA plugs kids into super-charged fun...

- The inside scoop on movie stars and athletes
- Hot, new video games and how to beat 'em
- The characters they love
- Stories about everyday kids
- *PLUS:* puzzles, contests, trivia, comics, and much, much more!

- -

☐ **YES!** Send me a FREE issue of **DISNEY ADVENTURES MAGAZINE.** (If my child loves it) I pay only $14.95 for the next 11 issues (12 in all). I save over $20 off the cover price. If we decide not to subscribe, I'll return the bill marked "cancel" and owe nothing. The FREE issue is ours to keep.

Mail your order to: DISNEY ADVENTURES
PO BOX 37284
Boone, IA 50037-0284

Child's Name _____ Birthday (optional):_____

Address _____

City _____ State _____ Zip _____

Parent's Signature _____

Payment enclosed _____ Bill me _____

Canadian and Foreign orders, please add $10 for postage and GST.
First issue will arrive within 4-8 weeks. Regular cover price is $2.99 per issue.

@ Disney   L1H1